Mini-Books and Manipulatives

BY DONALD M. SILVER

AND PATRICIA J. WYNNE

SCHOLASTIC
PROFESSIONAL BOOKS

NEW YORK • TORONTO • LONDON • AUCKLAND • SYDNEY
MEXICO CITY • NEW DELHI • HONG KONG

for Ronnie Levine,
my mother's friend and mine
—DS

To my mother,
who was always looking.
—PJW

Cover and interior art by Patricia J. Wynne
Cover and interior design by Kathy Massaro

ISBN: 0-590-68567-8

Contents

Introduction

Children are naturally curious. They want to find out what is happening in the world around them. They start by using their senses of sight, touch, hearing, smell, and even taste to explore their surroundings and learn about nature. Then come the questions that often start with "why" or "how." By the time children enter preschool or kindergarten, they're eager to learn by reading or by looking at pictures. These lift-and-look flap books and manipulatives have been designed so that they are easy to make and easy to read. Children get a sense of accomplishment from creating and coloring their very own mini-books and manipulatives. Each contains simple language and engaging pictures that help children gain confidence as readers. These activities also explain or reinforce discoveries children may already have made on their own. From learning how a spider spins its web to how the moon changes each month, children will be fascinated by this hands-on approach to learning.

What's Inside

This book is divided into five sections that cover a range of science topics. The lift-and-look projects are independent and can be used in any order. Within each chapter are lessons that feature the following:

OBJECTIVE What students will learn and accomplish

MEETING THE SCIENCE STANDARDS Identifies correlations with the National Science Education Standards

SCIENCE CORNER Summary of the science background information you need to teach the lesson

MAKING THE BOOK Easy-to-follow instructions with diagrams for assembling the models

TEACHING WITH THE BOOK Step-by-step lesson map (including discussion questions) for using the book to teach science concepts

MORE TO DO Related activities to extend learning

REPRODUCIBLE PAGES Ready-to-photocopy patterns for each lift-and-look project, which can be distributed to students

RESOURCES Related books and other media for students and teachers

Helpful Hints

As with any new instructional material, it's always a good idea to make the projects yourself before introducing them to your class. That way you can anticipate any questions that may arise and be ready to help your students as needed. When your students are ready to make theirs, you may want to model the steps for them and invite them to follow along. Or your finished book or manipulative can serve as a guide for students to study as they make their own books.

❧ The thickest black lines on the reproducible pages are Cut lines. Dotted lines on the reproducible pages are Fold lines.

❧ Some books have interior flaps that require cutting. An easy way to cut them is to use the "pinch method": Use your thumb and forefinger to fold the paper near one line and snip an opening. Then insert the scissors through the opening to easily cut out the flaps.

❧ If possible, enlarge the pattern pages to make the models easier for students to assemble.

❧ Some projects require double-sided copies. You may want to experiment with your copy machine to find the best way to position the pages in order to align them on both sides of the paper. If your photocopier cannot make double-sided copies, photocopy each side of the page and staple or glue together, back to back.

❧ If students will be coloring the books and using tape, have them color first so they won't have to color over the tape.

Encourage your students to bring their books and manipulatives home and share them with their families. You may also want to make extra copies to place in a learning center so that students can make and read them on their own.

We hope that you and your students get as much fun and excitement out of these lift-and-looks as we had in creating them. Enjoy!

Butterfly Pop-Up

Students make a pop-up book and observe
the changes a caterpillar goes through
as it metamorphoses into a butterfly.

Science Corner

Butterflies lay their eggs on plant leaves. When a caterpillar hatches out of an egg, it feeds almost continuously on leaves and plants. As the caterpillar gets bigger, it molts, or sheds, its skin and grows a new one. This molting happens several times, until the caterpillar is fully grown. When a caterpillar sheds its skin for the last time, a hard case called a chrysalis forms around its body. Inside the chrysalis, the caterpillar's body breaks down and transforms into an adult butterfly—with wings, scales, antennae, and six legs. After a few weeks, the butterfly emerges from its case. The new butterfly hangs upside down while its wings unfold and dry. The butterfly then takes off in search of sweet nectar for food and to look for a mate. Many butterflies live only a couple of weeks, while others may live several months.

MEETING THE SCIENCE STANDARDS

- Characteristics of Organisms
- Life Cycles of Organisms
- Organisms and Their Environments

MATERIALS

- reproducible pages 9 and 10
- scissors
- tape
- stapler
- colored pencils, crayons, or markers (optional)
- pocket mirrors (optional)

Making the Book

1 Photocopy pages 9 and 10. Color and cut out the three pieces with the solid black lines around them.

2 Fold pages 2 and 3 and pages 1 and 4 along the dotted lines so that the blank sides face each other inside. Nestle pages 2 and 3 inside pages 1 and 4 so that page 1 is on the outside. Staple the pages together as shown.

3 Open the book to the center and line up the left edge of the butterfly piece with the back of page 2 as shown. Tape the edges together. Repeat with the back of page 3 and the right edge of the butterfly.

4 Gently push the butterfly in toward the center fold of the book. Close the book and crease it.

Teaching With the Book

1 Draw an outline of a butterfly on the chalkboard and ask students to guess what it is. They may say it is a butterfly or a moth. Find out what students know about butterflies. Ask: "Are butterflies born with wings?" (*no*) "What are butterflies called when they are born?" (*caterpillars*) "What do they look like?" (*wormlike creatures*)

2 Invite students to color, assemble, and read their butterfly pop-up books. Let them decorate the blank pages opposite pages 2 and 3 with their own drawings of caterpillars and butterflies.

3 Ask: "What kind of animal are butterflies?" (*insects*) Explain to students that all insects have three body parts: head, thorax, and abdomen. Insects also have six legs, and most have wings and antennae. Invite students to turn to the back of their books to see the different parts of a butterfly's body. Have them compare the butterfly's features with those of the caterpillar.

4 Ask children to study the pop-up butterfly in the center of their book. What do they notice about the wings? (*They look the same on each side— they are symmetrical.*) Show students how they can tell if an object is symmetrical. Have them take turns placing a pocket mirror on the center of the butterfly. If they see the mirror image, the object is symmetrical. Let students use this method on pictures of different kinds of butterflies to find out if all butterfly wings are symmetrical. (See Resources, page 8.)

Resources

🌸 **The Butterfly Alphabet** by Kjell B. Sandved (Scholastic, 1998). Children will enjoy finding letters and numbers in the patterns on butterfly wings.

🌸 **The Children's Butterfly Site From the U.S. Geological Survey** www.mesc.nbs.gov/ butterfly/Butterfly. html

This Web site provides information about butterflies, answers frequently asked questions, and lists books, videos, and links to other Web sites with photographs of butterflies.

🌸 To order caterpillars, call Insect Lore at 1-800-LIVE-BUG or visit their Web site at www.insectlore.com

More to Do

Grow Your Own Butterfly

Students can witness firsthand the life cycle of a butterfly right in your own classroom. To build a butterfly habitat, use sharp scissors to cut off the top of an empty, clear, one-liter plastic bottle. Place a piece of cheesecloth over the open end. Use a rubber band to hold it in place. Add twigs and leaves for the caterpillar. You can order caterpillars from science supply catalogs. (See Resources, left, for more information.) Have students monitor their caterpillar every day and record their observations. When the butterfly emerges from its chrysalis, release the butterfly into your schoolyard or a nearby park.

Make a Butterfly

Make extra copies of the butterfly pattern in the lift-and-look book for each student. Invite students to make butterfly puppets using the pattern. Encourage them to color and decorate their butterflies. Then have students form a paper or pipe-cleaner ring big enough to fit the tip of their forefinger. Have them fold up the wings and then tape the butterfly's body to the ring. Students can wear their butterfly puppets and move their hands up and down to make the wings flap.

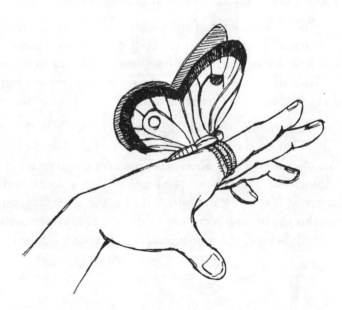

Butterfly Pop-Up Book

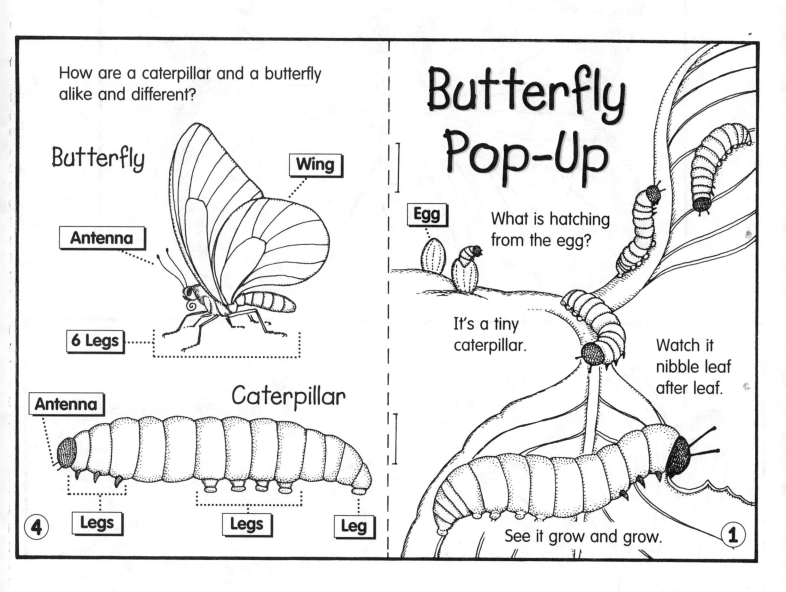

How are a caterpillar and a butterfly alike and different?

Butterfly

Wing

Antenna

6 Legs

Caterpillar

Antenna

Legs

Legs

Leg

④

Butterfly Pop-Up

Egg

What is hatching from the egg?

It's a tiny caterpillar.

Watch it nibble leaf after leaf.

See it grow and grow.

①

Lift & Look Science Mini-Books and Manipulatives
Scholastic Professional Books

Butterfly Pop-Up Book

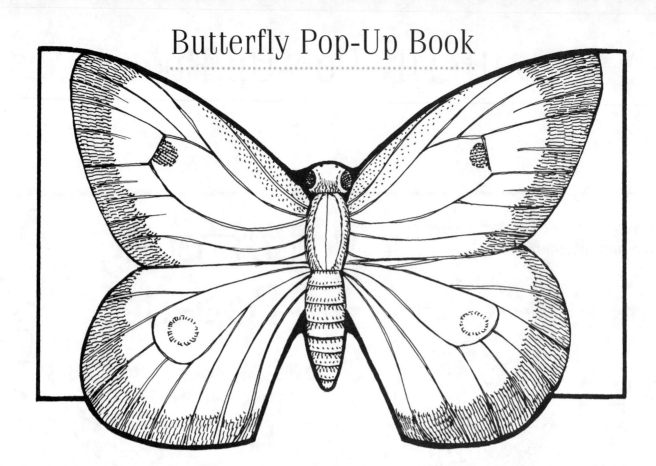

The butterfly sips sweet flower juice, called nectar.

One day the caterpillar stops growing.
A hard case, called a chrysalis, forms around it.

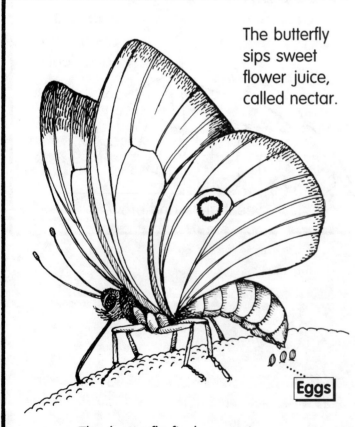

Eggs

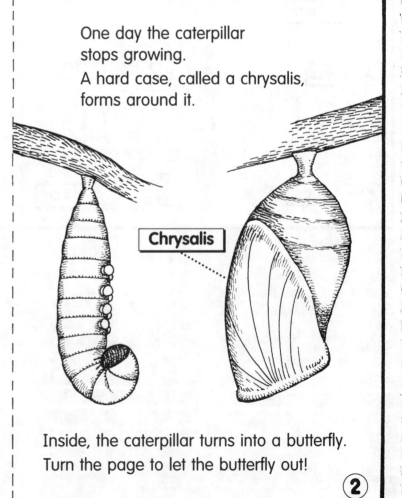

Chrysalis

The butterfly finds a mate.
Then it lays its eggs.
What will hatch from the eggs?

Inside, the caterpillar turns into a butterfly.
Turn the page to let the butterfly out!

③

②

The Spider's Web

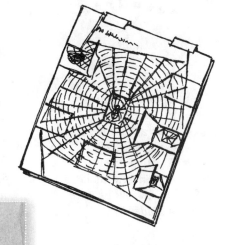

With this flap book, students find out how a spider spins a web and uses it to capture food.

Science Corner

There are more than 30,000 kinds of spiders, and all of them produce silk. Silk comes out as liquid from special glands in a spider's abdomen. The liquid hardens into thread when it touches air. Some silk threads are sticky; others are not. Spiders may use silk to make cases for their eggs, line their tunnels, build nests, or spin webs. A spider's web functions as a trap to catch insects and other creatures. A spider may sit on its web or hide nearby, attached to the web by a silk thread. When the web shakes, the spider can sense if the vibrations mean danger or food. If an insect is unfortunate enough to land on the web's sticky threads, the spider wraps the bug in silk and injects poison into its body. The poison paralyzes the prey and dissolves the bug's insides. The spider then sucks the liquid for food.

MEETING THE SCIENCE STANDARDS

- ◎ Characteristics of Organisms
- ◎ Life Cycles of Organisms
- ◎ Organisms and Their Environments

Making the Book

1 Photocopy pages 13 and 14.

2 Cut out the center window on page 13 along the solid black lines. Then cut the flaps.

3 Place page 13 over page 14 so that the sides line up.

4 Tape the sheets together at the top, bottom, and sides.

MATERIALS

- ◎ reproducible pages 13 and 14
- ◎ scissors
- ◎ tape
- ◎ colored pencils, crayons, or markers (optional)

✿ *Spider Spider*
by Kate Banks
(Farrar, Straus &
Giroux, 1996).
A young boy
imagines what he
would do if he were
a spider.

✿ *Spider's Web*
by Christine Back
and Barrie Watts
(Silver Burdett
Press, 1984).
Includes clear
diagrams of the
web-making
process and
extraordinary
photos of the
spider at work.

✿ http:www.yahooligans.
com/Science_and_
Nature/Living_Things_
Animals/Arachnids/
This Web site lists
informative
arachnid sites that
are appropriate for
children.

Teaching With the Book

1 Encourage students to share what they know about spiders. Ask: "Have you seen a spider? What did it look like?" List students' responses on the chalkboard.

2 Invite a volunteer to draw a spider on the board. Many people mistakenly think that spiders are insects. Explain to students that spiders are arachnids—they have eight legs, not six like adult insects. Unlike most insects, spiders lack wings and antennae. They have only two body sections (*head and abdomen*), whereas insects have three (*head, thorax, abdomen*).

3 Ask students: "Have you ever seen a spider's web? Where? What did it look like?" Inform students that spiderwebs come in different shapes—orb, funnel, tube, and so on. Students may be most familiar with the orb or circular webs.

4 Invite students to color, assemble, and read their books. Challenge them to answer the questions on the top page before they lift the flaps in numerical order to find the answers.

More to Do

Build a Web

Divide the class into groups of three or four students. Provide each group with scissors and a ball of yarn or string. Then challenge them to build a web. Students can make their web between the legs of a table or a chair, or between two rulers. Have students refer to their books as they make the frame, spokes, and spiral. Invite students to draw a spider or make one out of pipe cleaners and attach it to their web. They can also draw an insect and attach it to the web, or even wrap it in yarn or string to simulate spider silk.

Spider Play

Invite students to put together a play based on Eric Carle's classic *The Very Busy Spider* (Putnam & Grosset, 1984). Children can play the parts of different farm animals that come and watch as the spider builds its web. Encourage the student who plays the spider to either draw the spiderweb on the chalkboard or build one according to the instructions above.

The Spider's Web

How did the spider build its web?
Lift flaps 1, 2, and 3 to find out.

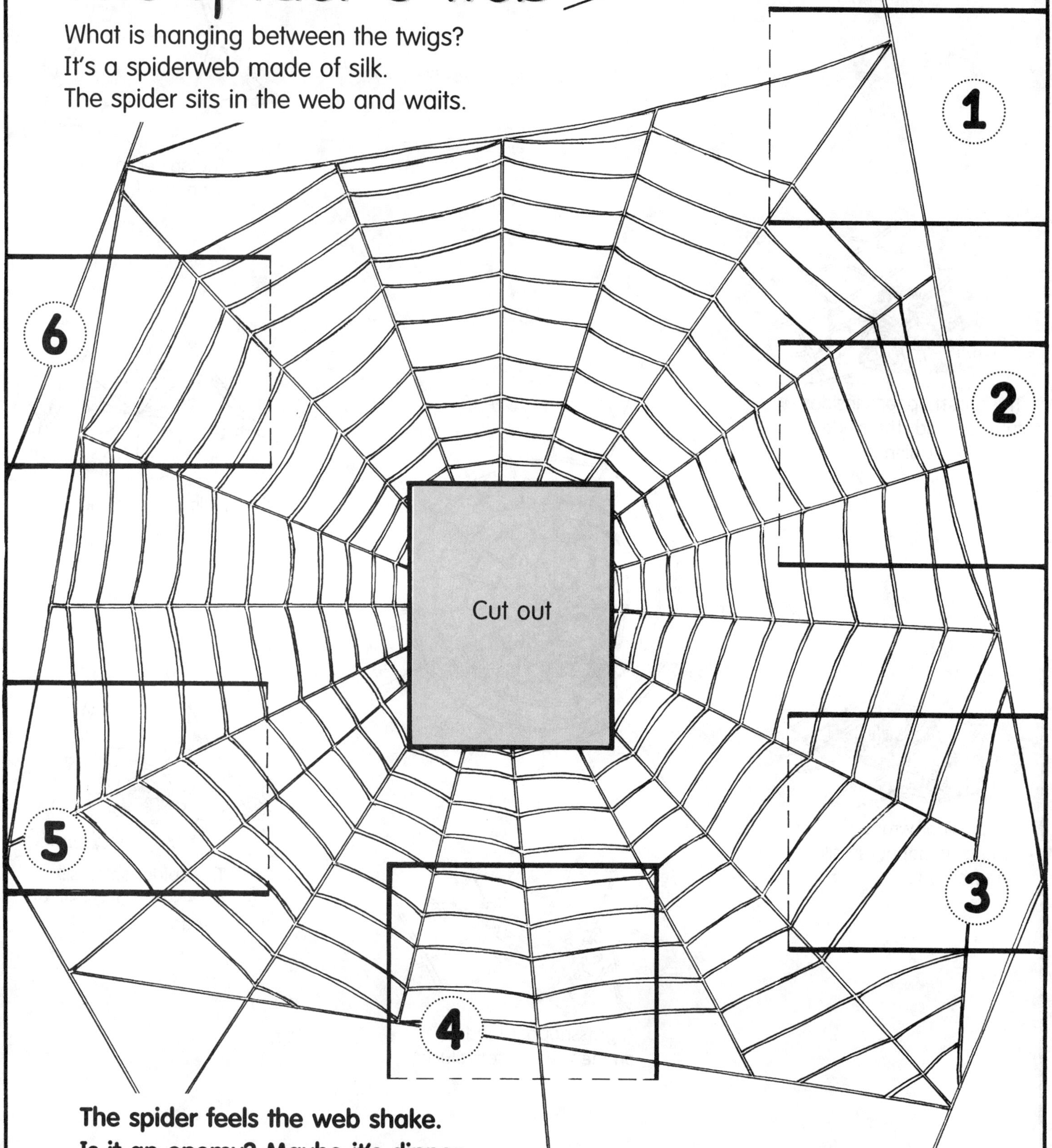

What is hanging between the twigs?
It's a spiderweb made of silk.
The spider sits in the web and waits.

1

6

2

Cut out

5

3

4

The spider feels the web shake.
Is it an enemy? Maybe it's dinner.
Lift flaps 4, 5, and 6 to see what the
spider does.

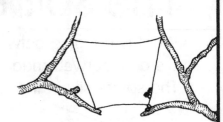

The spider makes
a frame of silk.

The grasshopper's insides
turn to liquid. The spider
drinks it for dinner.

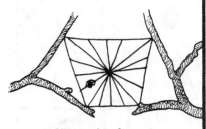

It fills in the frame
with silk threads.

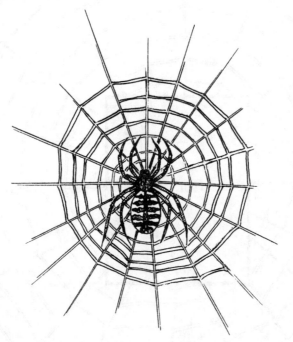

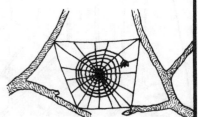

The spider spins silk
circles and adds sticky
threads.

The spider wraps
the grasshopper in silk
and bites it.

A grasshopper lands
on the web. It gets stuck.

Life & Look Science™ Mini-Books and Manipulatives   Scholastic Professional Books™

Glide, Squirrel, Glide!

Students make a bookmark to learn how a flying squirrel glides from one tree to another to escape an enemy.

Science Corner

Flying squirrels can't really fly. Instead, they glide through the air for distances up to 150 feet (46 meters). Technically, they should be called gliding squirrels. When a flying squirrel leaps from a high branch of a tall tree, it spreads its four legs and stretches the skin flaps along the sides of its body. Once in the air, the squirrel uses its flat tail and legs to help it steer. When the squirrel approaches a tree to land, it raises its body and its tail. Its skin flaps then break its speed so the squirrel can slow down and grip the trunk with its sharp claws. Flying squirrels are found in forests of North America, Europe, and Asia. They are active mainly at night, when they search for nuts, seeds, and insects to eat.

MEETING THE SCIENCE STANDARDS

◎ Characteristics of Organisms

◎ Organisms and Their Environments

Making the Bookmark

1 Photocopy pages 17 and 18.

2 Cut out the two squirrel tail and bookmark pieces along the solid black outer lines. Tape each set together back to back.

3 Tape the tail to the squirrel's body.

4 Hold the squirrel piece so that the eyes are on top. Poke a hole through the black dot as shown.

MATERIALS

◎ reproducible pages 17 and 18

◎ scissors

◎ tape

◎ two-foot-long piece of yarn or string

◎ paper clip

◎ colored pencils, crayons, or markers (optional)

✿ **Flying Squirrel at Acorn Place** by Barbara Gaines Winkelman (Soundprints, 1998). This book and accompanying audiocassette follow a night in the life of a flying squirrel as it searches for a place to nest, hunts for food, and avoids enemies.

✿ *Night Gliders* by Joanne Ryder (Bridgewater Books, 1996). Young readers get a close-up look at flying squirrels as they glide from tree to tree in their nightly search for food.

5 Slide the paper clip over the top of the bookmark, as shown, and tape it in place.

6 Tie a loop in one end of the string, as shown. Thread the other end of the string through the hole in the squirrel. Tie a fat knot about halfway down from the loop on the other side of the squirrel. Tie the unlooped end to the paper clip.

Teaching With the Book

1 Have students think about different ways they move from one place to another. (*walk, run, swim, hop, and so on*) Make a list on the chalkboard. Then challenge students to name animals that also move in these ways. List their responses next to the movement words.

2 Explain to students that some animals can move in ways that people can't. For example, people can't fly. We need airplanes and other flying machines to help us take to the air. Ask: "Which animals can fly?" (*birds, bats, and many insects*)

3 Inform students that some animals may look like they're flying, but they don't have actual wings. Instead, these animals glide through the air. One of these animals is the flying squirrel. Ask students: "How do squirrels get around?" (*Many squirrels run on the ground, climb trees, and leap from tree to tree.*) "Have you ever seen a squirrel leap from branch to branch or from tree to tree?"

4 Invite students to color, assemble, and read their bookmarks. Students can fold their squirrels along the dotted lines and then open them to show how the skin flaps stretch when the squirrel glides.

More to Do

Control That Fall

Flying squirrels use their skin flaps to control how fast they fall. The flaps catch the air and slow the animal's descent. A parachute works the same way. Have students make a parachute using an   8-inch square sheet of paper, four 8-inch pieces of string, tape, and two rolled-up balls of paper. Tape one end of each string to the paper as shown. Tape the other end to one paper ball. Have students hold the second paper ball in one hand and the parachute in the other. Tell students to lift their arms as high as they can and drop the ball and parachute at the same time. Which takes longer to fall? (*the parachute*)

Glide, Squirrel, Glide!

Watch out, flying squirrel.
A hungry owl is nearby.

Quick!
Spread your legs.
Stretch your skin flaps.
Glide to another tree.

↑

① 1

Lift & Look Science Mini-Books and Manipulatives   Scholastic Professional Books

Glide,
Squirrel,
Glide!

Glide, Squirrel, Glide!

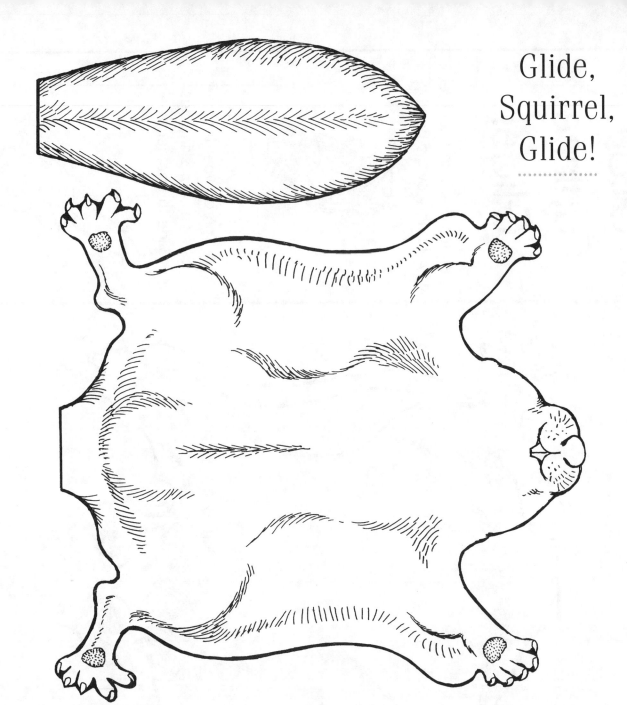

There's the tree.
Now, raise your body
and tail.

Grab the trunk
with your sharp claws
and land.

Hurry to the
other side of
the trunk.

The owl
won't find you there.
You're safe!

Inside a Beaver Lodge

Students look inside a beaver lodge and find out where and how beavers build their homes.

Science Corner

Beavers build their home or lodge in still ponds, also called beaver ponds. To create these ponds, beavers erect dams across fast-flowing streams or rivers. The dams hold back the water, slowing it down and causing it to rise. Soon the water is high enough to build a lodge. To make their lodge, beavers stack piles of wood and cement them with earth and mud. Inside the lodge, above the water line, is a big chamber where the beavers live. A small opening at the top of the lodge brings in fresh air for breathing. Beavers enter and leave their lodge through two underwater tunnels that lead in and out of the living chamber. Near one of the tunnel openings, beavers store tree branches for food in the winter.

MEETING THE SCIENCE STANDARDS

- Characteristics of Organisms
- Life Cycles of Organisms
- Organisms and Their Environments

Making the Book

1 Photocopy pages 21 and 22. Cut along the outer black lines on each page. Cut the flaps along the heavy black lines. Use the pinch method (see page 5) to cut the flap around the lodge.

2 Place page 21 on top of page 22 so that the pages are aligned.

3 Fold both sheets in half along the center horizontal dotted line. Crease with your thumb.

4 Fold again along the center vertical dotted line. With the title page of the book facing you, crease the side fold.

5 Open the book and pull the beaver lodge forward. Crease as shown in the diagram at the top of this page.

MATERIALS

- reproducible pages 21 and 22
- scissors
- colored pencils, crayons, or markers (optional)

Teaching With the Book

1 Bring in pictures of different animal homes—a bird's nest, a beehive, or a termite mound. Have students think about animal homes—what they look like, where they can be found, how animals build them, and so on. Share the pictures with students to help them get a better sense of where different animals live.

2 Find out what students know about beavers' homes. Ask: "What does a beaver's home look like?" (*a pile of sticks, usually in the middle of a pond*) Inform students that a beaver's home is also called a lodge.

3 Invite students to color, assemble, and read their flap books.

4 When students lift the flap on the cover page, they will see an underwater tunnel that leads to the beaver lodge. When they open their books, students will see two tunnels that lead in and out of the lodge. Explain to students that animals larger than beavers cannot fit through the tunnels. Ask: "Why might this be important to beavers?" (*Predators can't enter the lodge.*)

5 On page 4, students will read about how a beaver uses other parts of its body to build a home. For example, a beaver uses its tail and webbed feet to swim and to carry sticks to its lodge. Inform students that a beaver's front teeth keep growing throughout its life. Munching through hard wood helps to wear down its teeth so they don't grow too long.

More to Do

Busy as Beavers

Students can't really appreciate a beaver's building expertise until they try to build a lodge themselves. Collect twigs and branches, and challenge your students to build a mini beaver lodge using the picture in their books as a guide. (If they prefer, children can try their hand at building a beaver dam in a plastic dishpan.) When students are finished building, test the strength of their structure: Have students push a pencil through holes in their lodges. What happens? Inform students that beavers fill the holes in their dams or lodges with mud to keep water out. In winter, the mud covering a beaver lodge freezes solid and keeps out foxes and other predators that can reach the lodge by walking across the frozen pond.

In a "People House"

Houses around the world look very different from each other. Have students look through old magazines and bring in pictures of different homes. Encourage students to compare their own homes with those in the pictures. Ask: "How are they different? How are they alike?"

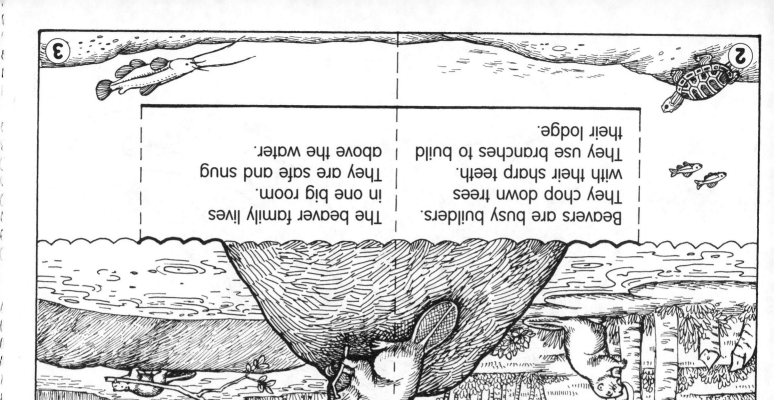

③

Beavers build dams to hold back water.

The beaver family lives in one big room. They are safe and snug above the water.

Beavers are busy builders. They chop down trees with their sharp teeth. They use branches to build their lodge.

②

How does a beaver use its body parts to build a home?

Sharp Teeth

Webbed Feet and Flat Tail

Front Paws

④

Inside a Beaver Lodge

What is in the middle of the pond? It's a beaver house, called a lodge. How do the beavers get in and out? Lift the flap and look.

①

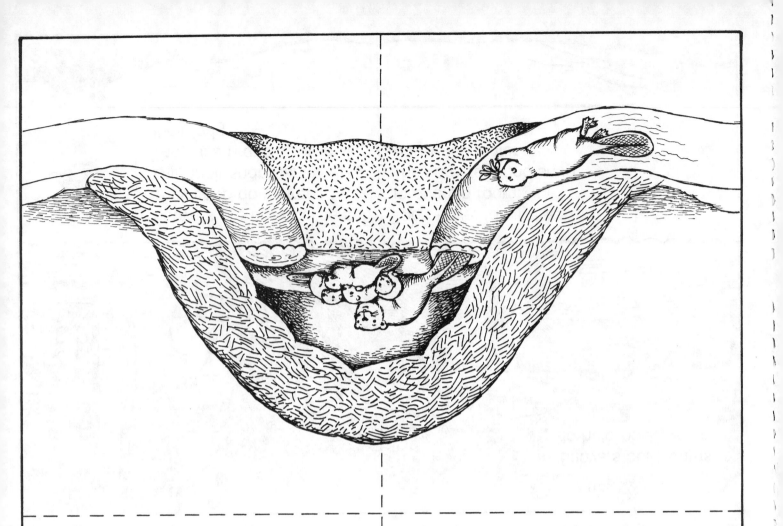

A beaver's front teeth can cut down trees.

A beaver's webbed feet and flat tail help it swim as it carries sticks to its lodge.

A beaver's front paws help it pick up sticks to build with.

Beavers enter and leave through an underwater tunnel.

Lift & Look Science Mini-Books and Manipulatives   Scholastic Professional Books

Plant Helpers

Students learn how different animals and the wind help plants make seeds.

Science Corner

Pollination is the process of carrying pollen (tiny yellowish grains) from one flower to another so plants can make seeds. Agents, such as animals, people, or even the wind, that transport pollen are called pollinators. People often deliberately transfer pollen from one flower to another to breed plants. But natural pollinators don't help plants on purpose. For instance, the wind just blows and spreads pollen by chance. As animals feed on a flower's sweet nectar or pollen, some pollen grains stick to their beaks, fur, feathers, wings, legs, or other body parts. When the animals visit another flower, some of the pollen grains drop into or touch that flower's reproductive organs. The flower can then start making seeds.

MEETING THE SCIENCE STANDARDS

◎ Characteristics of Organisms
◎ Life Cycles of Organisms
◎ Organisms and Their Environments

Making the Book

1 Make a double-sided photocopy of pages 25 and 26. Or use the arrows to align single pages as exactly as possible and glue them back to back.

2 With the question side (outside) faceup, cut out the six-section piece along the solid black lines.

3 Turn the piece over so you can see the animals. Fold the book's six sections, or "petals," toward the center along the dotted line. (The order does not matter.)

4 Turn the book over so that the title, PLANT HELPERS, is on top.

MATERIALS

◎ reproducible pages 25 and 26
◎ scissors
◎ gluestick (optional)
◎ colored pencils, crayons, or markers (optional)

Teaching With the Book

1 Bring in different kinds of seeds, such as apple, pumpkin, and orange, and show them to students. Ask: "What do you think these are? Where do you think seeds come from?" (*fruits or cones*) Explain to students that fruits come from flowers, and flowers make seeds that can grow into new plants.

2 Invite students to color and assemble their lift-and-look flap books. When reading their books, have students start on the title page and lift each flap.

3 When students reach the book's center, they will discover that plant helpers carry pollen grains from one plant to another. (The pollen grain shown is greatly enlarged. In reality, most pollen grains can fit on the head of a pin.) Inform students that flowers have male and female parts. Pollen grains are made in a flower's male parts. The grains have to reach another flower's female parts so the flower can form seeds. Explain that, for seeds to grow, pollen from one kind of flower must reach the same kind of flower. If pollen lands on a different kind of flower, nothing will happen.

4 Tell students that some plants don't make their seeds in flowers. Pine trees and other conifers, for example, develop pollen and seeds inside cones. The wind carries pollen from one pine tree to another.

More to Do

What's in a Flower?

Bring in simple flowers, such as tulips, apple blossoms, or lilies, and invite students to take them apart. (Florists often provide slightly aged flowers for educational purposes at no charge.) Encourage students to use hand lenses to take a closer look at a flower. Use the picture at right to point out a flower's parts.

Stamens are stalks that hold pollen.

The **pistil** is the stalk on which pollen must fall so that a flower can make seeds.

Sepals protect the flower.

Petals attract insects and other pollinators with their colors and patterns.

Take a cotton swab and touch the stamens to pick up some pollen. (NOTE: Some students may be allergic to pollen and should not get it on their fingers or breathe it in.) Explain to students that most flowers do not self-pollinate. Their stamens are separate from and often lower than the pistil.

Traveling Seeds

Like pollen, seeds need help to reach good growing grounds. Some seeds may hitch a ride on animals or people, while others may blow in the wind or float on water. Give students each a popcorn kernel and tell them that this is their seed. Challenge students to create something that would help their seed travel at least five feet away. Provide materials such as paper, string, cotton balls, and glue.

Plant Helpers

What helps this daisy make seeds?

What helps this hibiscus make seeds?

What helps this grass make seeds?

Plant Helpers

Plants need helpers to make seeds. Seeds grow into new plants. Plants get help in different ways. How? Turn your book over and lift the flaps.

What helps this clover make seeds?

What helps this goldenrod make seeds?

What helps this cactus make seeds?

Plant Helpers

Inside

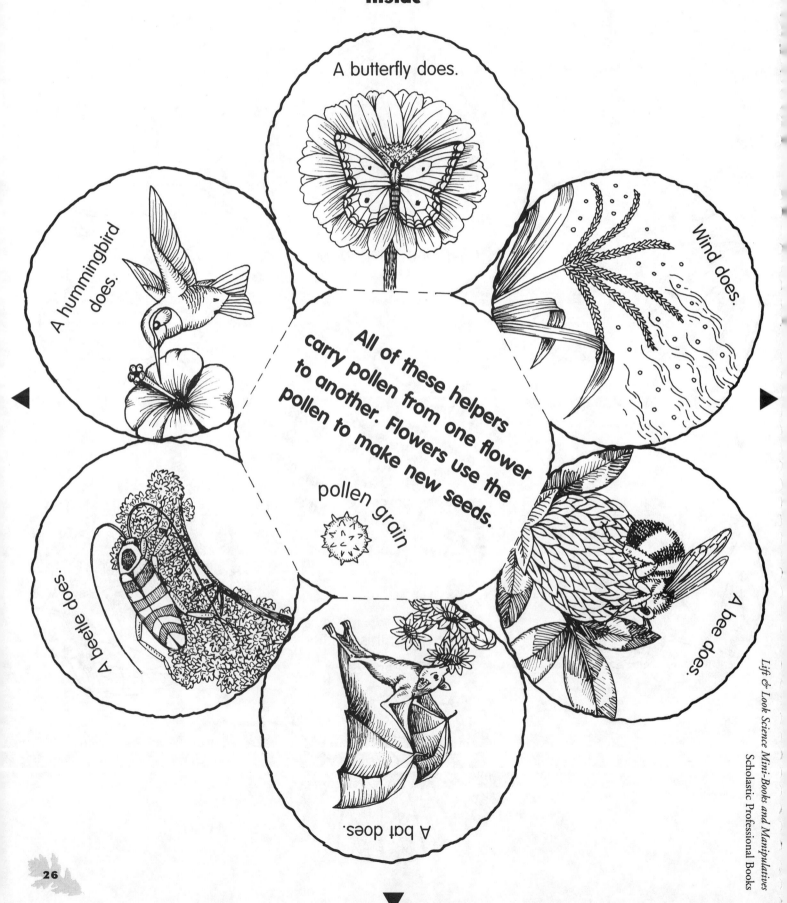

A butterfly does.

A hummingbird does.

Wind does.

A beetle does.

A bee does.

A bat does.

All of these helpers carry pollen from one flower to another. Flowers use the pollen to make new seeds.

pollen grain

Life & Look Science Mini-Books and Manipulatives
Scholastic Professional Books

Grow an Oak Tree

As students unfold this book, they discover how a giant oak tree grows from a tiny acorn.

Most people think of acorns as ordinary nuts. But acorns are actually fruits that contain seeds from which oak trees grow. Acorns drop from oak trees before the leaves fall in autumn. Those seeds that are not eaten by squirrels and other animals have a chance of sprouting. When a seed begins to sprout, a root splits open the acorn's hard shell and pushes its way into the ground. The root branches out and soaks up water from the ground. Soon the plant's stem and leaves grow toward the sun. Leaves make food for the plant using energy from the sun, carbon dioxide from the air, and water from the soil. It takes many years for an acorn to turn into a fullgrown oak tree.

MEETING THE SCIENCE STANDARDS

◎ Characteristics of Organisms
◎ Life Cycles of Organisms

Making the Book

1 Make a double-sided photocopy of pages 29 and 30. Or use the arrows to align single copies as exactly as possible and glue them together back to back.

2 Cut along the heavy black line on page 29. Place the grown oak tree (page 30) faceup on a flat surface.

3 Fold page 30 in half along the dotted lines as shown. Then fold the leaf sides together into the center.

4 Fold at the center so that the title, GROW AN OAK TREE, faces you.

MATERIALS

◎ reproducible pages 29 and 30
◎ scissors
◎ gluestick (optional)
◎ colored pencils, crayons, or markers (optional)

* **The Gift of the Tree** by Alvin Tresselt (Lothrop, Lee & Shepard, 1992). What happens after a tree dies? Students learn that even after an oak tree dies, it can still provide shelter to many animals.

* **The Tree** by Gallimard Jeunesse and Pascale De Bourgoing (Scholastic, 1992). Transparent pages add to the charm of this book that follows a tree through all its stages of life and through the changing seasons.

5 Fold the two ends in along the dotted lines so that they meet at the center crease as shown.

6 Press down firmly and fold at the center crease again so that the title is on top of the lift-and-look book.

Teaching With the Book

1 Ask students: "What's the biggest tree you've ever seen? How big was it?" Explain that most trees, no matter how big, grow from small seeds. Although most trees grow slowly, some can eventually reach heights of 50 to 100 feet.

2 Invite students to color and assemble their books. To read their book, students open the folds in stages, as shown.

3 As students unfold their book, ask them to describe what they see on each page. Ask: "What has changed?" Have students identify and label the different parts of the tree as they appear.

4 Inform students that acorns are also food for many animals, including squirrels. These animals gather the nuts that fall on the ground and store them for winter. Some squirrels may bury the acorns, then retrieve them later. Ask students: "What do you think might happen if a squirrel forgets where it buried an acorn?" (*The acorn might grow into a new oak tree.*)

More to Do

Home, Tree, Home

Find a tree on the school grounds or in the park. Invite students to search for signs of animals that live in and around the tree. For example, do they see fallen leaves, acorns, or seeds on the ground that have been munched by squirrels, chipmunks, or other animals? Bring along hand lenses so that children can check the tree bark for crawling creatures or for holes in which beetles may live. Challenge them to search for scratches on bark left by animals in search of seeds, fruits, and other food on the branches. Also encourage students to lie on the ground and look up for bird nests, squirrels, or other tree life. Suggest that they listen for sounds, too, such as buzzing or chirping.

In autumn,

Give it water
and watch it grow
into an oak tree.

See it sprout.

②

④

(Open) →

oak leaves fall.

Grow an Oak Tree

Plant an acorn.

①

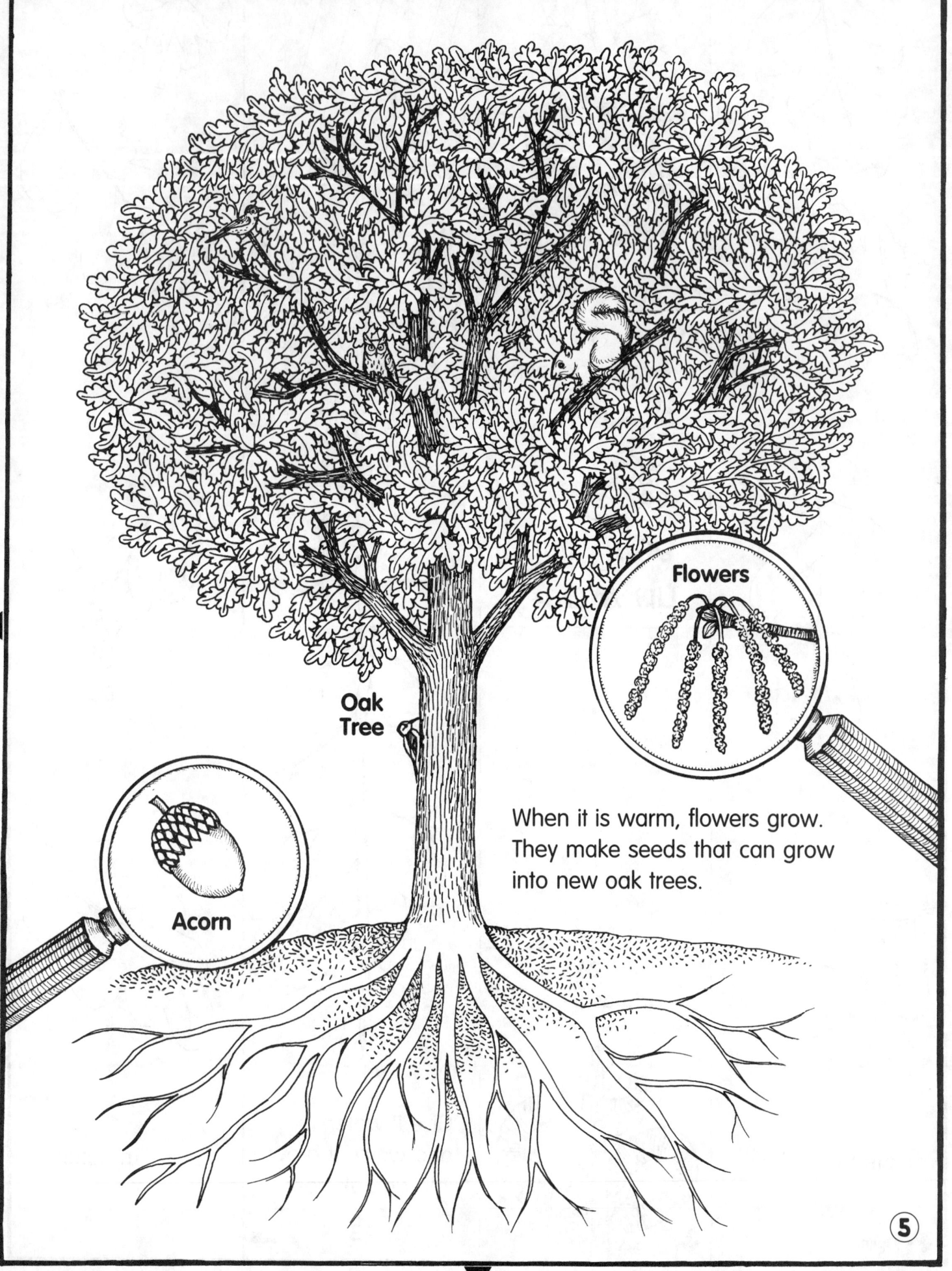

Flowers

Oak Tree

Acorn

When it is warm, flowers grow.
They make seeds that can grow
into new oak trees.

The Backyard Book

Students identify daytime and nighttime animals that live in the backyard or park.

Science Corner

A habitat is a place where a community of animals and plants live together and depend on one another for survival. Some habitats, such as backyards and parks, are small, whereas others, such as rain forests and oceans, are huge. Regardless of its size, a habitat contains all the essential things organisms need to survive. Plants make their own food using energy from the sun. In turn, some animals eat plants to get energy, and some animals eat other animals. Rain provides water for both plants and animals. Breathable oxygen is everywhere. Rocks, trees, and even soil provide homes and shelter for animals.

MEETING THE SCIENCE STANDARDS

◎ Characteristics of Organisms
◎ Life Cycles of Organisms
◎ Organisms and Their Environments

Making the Book

1 Photocopy pages 33 and 34. Cut out the patterns along the outer solid black lines. Then cut off the text strips at the edge of each sheet along the solid black lines.

2 Fold the remaining parts of each pattern along the center dotted lines.

3 Cut along the solid black lines on the DAY and NIGHT pattern (page 33) to open the six flaps.

MATERIALS

◎ reproducible pages 33 and 34
◎ scissors
◎ tape
◎ colored pencils, crayons, and markers (optional)

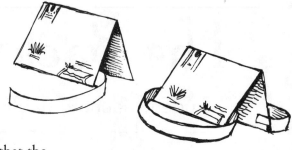

4 Tape the DAYTIME IN THE BACKYARD text strip to the bottom of the INSIDE (DAY) pattern as shown.

5 Repeat on the other side with the NIGHTTIME IN THE BACKYARD text strip.

6 Place page 33 on top of page 34 so that the arrows on each page are aligned. Tuck each side behind the taped text strips.

7 Tape the sheets together around the edges. Be careful not to tape down a flap.

Teaching With the Book

1 Ask students to think about animals they've seen in their backyard or local park. Ask: "What were the animals doing?" Make a list on the chalkboard.

2 Challenge students to think about what backyard animals need to stay alive. (*Animals need food, water, air to breathe, and safe places to hide, sleep, and raise their young.*) List students' responses on the board. Explain to students that a habitat is a place where animals and plants live and can find all the things they need to survive. Ask students: "What habitats can you think of?" (*forests, parks, lakes, and so on*) Inform students that their own backyard or local park is a habitat, too.

3 Invite students to color, assemble, and read their lift-and-look flap books. Then ask: "What do you think the animals you see in the daytime do at night?" (*go to sleep*) Explain to students that, like people, many animals are active during the day and rest at night. But other animals do just the opposite: They sleep during the day and scurry about at night in search of food. When students lift the flaps on the day scene, they will see where night creatures hide by day. Flaps on the night scene reveal where day creatures sleep.

More to Do

Use Your Senses

How do nighttime animals find their way about in the dark? Turn off the lights in your classroom or have children close their eyes. Ask: "When you can't see very well, which senses tell you what's going on around you?" (*hearing, smell, and touch*) Inform students that bats emit high-frequency sounds to locate objects. These sounds bounce off different things and echo back to a bat's ears. These echoes tell a bat where it is safe to fly and where a moth or other tasty insect can be found. Have students research how other nighttime animals use their senses in the dark.

Daytime in the Backyard

The backyard looks very busy.
Lots of animals are hungry.

The earthworm lifts
a leaf to eat.

A bat swoops down
to catch a moth.

Fireflies
blink
their
lights on
and off.

Night

Day

The squirrel
looks for a nut.

The little lizard suns
itself to keep warm.

The butterfly
sips sweet nectar
from a flower.

Where are the creatures
that come out at night?
Lift the flaps and see.

Fireflies hide
in the grass.

The earthworm rests in its
underground tunnel.

The bat sleeps
in a tree hole.

Nighttime in the Backyard

The sun has set. It is night.
Animals hunt by the light of the moon.

The squirrel sleeps
in its nest.

Where are the animals
that come out during the day?
Lift the flaps and find out.

The butterfly hides
on a plant.

The lizard spends
the night under a
pile of leaves.

Inside (Night)

Lift & Look Science Mini-Books and Manipulatives —Scholastic Professional Books

What Lives in a Pond?

Students discover how some animals have adapted to living in a pond.

Science Corner

A pond is a small body of water found on land. Pond water is fresh, not salty like seawater. It is also shallow enough for sunlight to reach the pond bottom. A pond is home to all sorts of plants and animals, such as insects, amphibians, and fish.

MEETING THE SCIENCE STANDARDS

- Characteristics of Organisms
- Life Cycles of Organisms
- Organisms and Their Environments

Making the Book

1 Make a double-sided copy of pages 37 and 38. Or use the arrows to align single copies as exactly as possible and glue them together back to back.

2 Cut out the pattern along the outer solid black lines.

3 Fold the pattern along the horizontal dotted line so that the title page faces you.

4 Cut open the four flaps along the solid black lines, using the pinch method shown on page 5.

5 Tape the folded page in half, as shown.

MATERIALS

- reproducible pages 37 and 38
- gluestick (optional)
- scissors
- tape
- colored pencils, crayons, or markers (optional)

Resources

✿ **In the Small, Small Pond** by Denise Fleming (Henry Holt, 1993). Brightly colored illustrations and simple text introduce young readers to pond dwellers that change from season to season.

✿ **One Small Square: Pond** by Donald M. Silver and Patricia J. Wynne (Freeman and Co., 1994). Readers take a look at a pond and its inhabitants, one small section at a time.

✿ **Pond Seasons** by Sue A. Alderson (Publishers Group West, 1997). Through poems and evocative watercolor illustrations, readers explore the seasonal changes that occur in a pond.

Teaching With the Book

1 Find out how many students have seen a pond. Ask: "Where have you seen a pond? What did it look like? What lives in it?"

2 Invite students to color and assemble their lift-and-look flap book.

3 Have students read the questions on the flaps one at a time. Encourage them to lift the flap and try to figure out the answer by looking at the picture first. Then have them read the text on the underside of the flap.

4 Challenge students to think of other things that live in a pond, such as plants like water lilies and animals like salamanders.

More to Do

Indoor Pond

If you don't have a nearby pond for the class to visit, make one right in your own classroom. Set up a small wading pool on top of a plastic tarp in one corner of your classroom. Fill the pool with about three inches of tap water and let it sit for 24 hours. Collect two buckets of pond water, including the bottom muck, floating plants, sticks, and rocks. Empty the buckets into the pool and let the water settle for a couple of days. Invite children to look for aquatic life in your indoor pond. Help them use plastic spoons to turn over rocks and sticks. Have students keep a science journal to record their observations. After about a week, return the contents of the pool to an outdoor pond.

A Frog's Life

Draw students' attention to the tadpole picture in their books and then to the frog under the flap. Challenge them to think about how a tadpole changes as it becomes an adult frog—for example, a tadpole loses its tail, grows legs, and so on. Explain that a frog is an amphibian—a vertebrate (animal with a backbone) that has no hair, scales, feathers, or claws. It usually lives the first part of its life in water and the rest on land. Frogs lay eggs in water. The eggs hatch into tadpoles that live underwater. Within a few weeks, tadpoles metamorphose, or change, into adult frogs that live on land. Have students draw a picture of the three stages in a frog's life (*egg, tadpole, adult*). Invite them to find out how a tadpole and a frog breathe.

What Lives in a Pond?

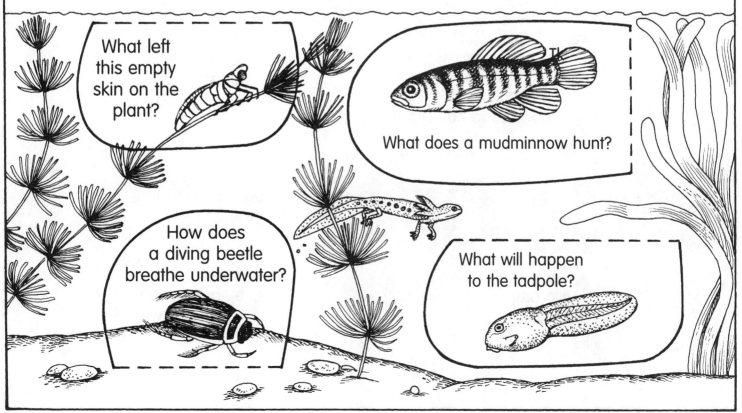

What left this empty skin on the plant?

What does a mudminnow hunt?

How does a diving beetle breathe underwater?

What will happen to the tadpole?

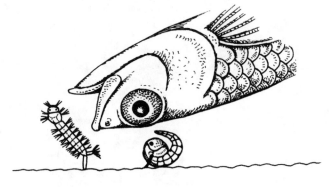

It hunts for
mosquitoes or
tadpoles to eat.

It's a grown-up
dragonfly ready
to fly away.

It will grow
into a frog.

It carries
an air bubble
when it dives.

Life & Look Science Mini-Books and Manipulatives   Scholastic Professional Books

Life in the Sea

Students find out how various animals
are adapted to living in different layers of the sea.

If you could drain the water from the world's oceans, you would see towering mountains and deep canyons on the ocean floor. Extending hundreds of miles from the seashore is the continental shelf, the shallowest part of the ocean. Even though it makes up only 10 percent of the ocean floor, the continental shelf provides most of the fish we eat. Tiny one-celled plants, called phytoplankton, are the basis of the ocean's food chain. These tiny plants make food using energy from sunlight. In turn, single-celled animals eat phytoplankton. These animals are eaten by small fish, which are then eaten by larger fish, and so on.

About 300 feet below the surface, the ocean becomes very dim. Little sunlight can penetrate the water. Sharks and other large fish that live here hunt in surface waters.

Sunlight cannot reach depths of 4,000 feet or more. Few animals can live in the near-freezing waters above the deep-sea floor. Many of the animals that live here produce their own light. There is little food available besides the bits and pieces of dead sea life that slowly drift down from above.

MEETING THE SCIENCE STANDARDS

- ◎ Characteristics of Organisms
- ◎ Life Cycles of Organisms
- ◎ Organisms and Their Environments

MATERIALS

- ◎ reproducible page 41
- ◎ scissors
- ◎ colored pencils, crayons, or markers (optional)
- ◎ blue cellophane or blue tissue paper and tape (optional)

Making the Book

1 Photocopy page 41. Cut out the pattern along the outer solid black lines.

2 Fold the sheet along the two dotted lines so that page 1 is in front, page 2 is in the middle, and page 3 is at the back.

3 Cut along the solid black lines on page 1 to open the three flaps.

✿ **Commotion in the Ocean** by Giles Andreae (Little Tiger Press, 1998). Colorful illustrations introduce various animals that live in different parts of the sea.

✿ **I Wonder Why the Sea Is Salty** by Anita Ganeri (Kingfisher, 1995). This vividly illustrated book gives simple answers to children's questions about the bottom of the sea, waves, the fastest fish, and other ocean wonders.

✿ **The Magic School Bus on the Ocean Floor** by Joanna Cole (Scholastic, 1992). The Friz and her class dive into the ocean to learn about animal and plant life, a coral reef, and much more.

4 OPTIONAL: Tape a piece of blue cellophane or blue tissue paper over the DARKNESS zone on page 1 to indicate that no sunlight reaches those depths.

Teaching With the Book

1 Introduce the lesson by displaying a map of the world. Ask students: "Is the earth mostly land or water?" (*Water covers more than two thirds of the earth.*)

2 Have students describe what they know about the ocean. List key words on the chalkboard, such as *waves, fish, saltwater, tides,* and so on.

3 Ask: "What kinds of animals live in the sea?" Make a list on the board. Explain that some sea animals live near the ocean's surface, while others live in the deepest, darkest parts of the ocean. The ocean gets deeper as the distance from land increases. In some places, the ocean is more than five miles (eight kilometers) deep.

4 Invite students to color, assemble, and read their lift-and-look flap books.

5 As they read the first page, students will learn that the ocean has three layers, or zones: *sunlight, twilight,* and *darkness.* Invite students to open each flap to read about each zone. Then challenge them to identify and label the different creatures they see in each zone, using the Field Guide on page 3.

More to Do

What Is It?

To classify means to put things into groups. One way to classify sea life is according to where in the ocean it lives. Challenge students to come up with other ways to classify sea life. For instance, big or small animals; floaters, swimmers, crawlers, or flyers; and so on. Help students research and report on an animal that lives in the sea. Students should try to find out what kind of animal it is (fish, mammal, mollusk, and so on), what it eats, how it moves, and so on. Based on students' reports, encourage the class to brainstorm more ways to classify sea life. Draw a Venn diagram on the chalkboard, and invite students to group their animals in each circle.

Web of Life

Whether on land or at sea, plants and animals are part of a food chain—an arrangement of organisms according to the order in which each uses the next as a food source. Using the animals featured in their books, students can try to identify the various food chains in the ocean. Students may draw arrows to indicate which animal eats which.

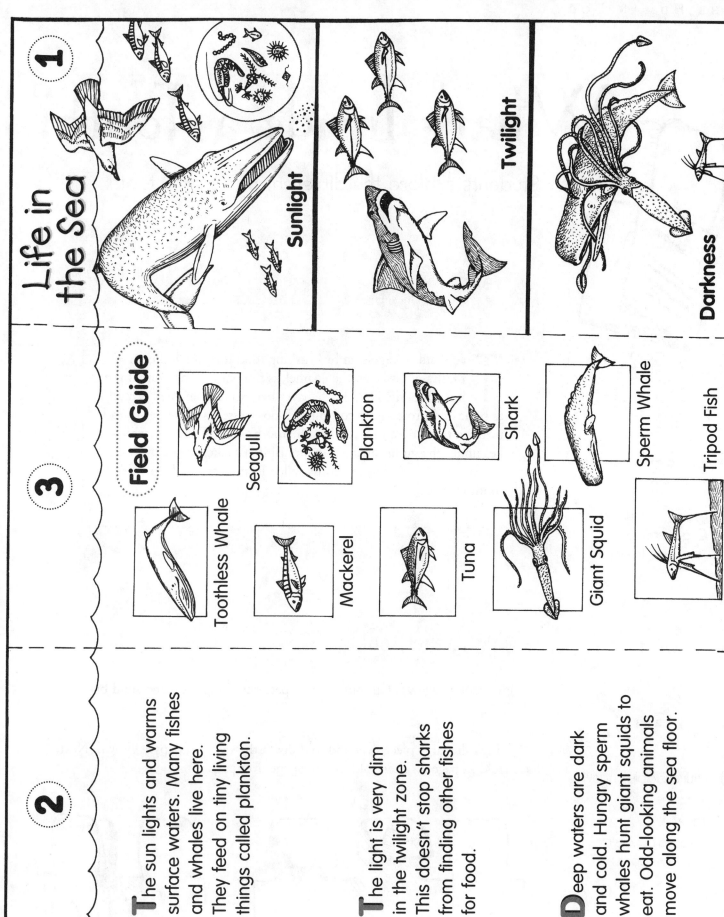

Life in the Sea

1

Sunlight

Twilight

Darkness

3

Field Guide

Seagull

Plankton

Shark

Sperm Whale

Toothless Whale

Mackerel

Tuna

Giant Squid

Tripod Fish

2

The sun lights and warms surface waters. Many fishes and whales live here. They feed on tiny living things called plankton.

The light is very dim in the twilight zone. This doesn't stop sharks from finding other fishes for food.

Deep waters are dark and cold. Hungry sperm whales hunt giant squids to eat. Odd-looking animals move along the sea floor.

What's Inside a Tooth?

Students explore the different parts of a tooth.

Science Corner

Teeth aid in digestion by crushing food into small pieces. A tooth's outer layer, the enamel, is the hardest material in the human body. Dentin, the layer beneath the enamel, is hard as bone and protects the soft pulp. Blood vessels and nerves thread through the pulp and extend to the tooth's root. The root, which lies under the gums, anchors the tooth in a socket in the jawbone. Natural cement and tough cords called ligaments also help hold the tooth in place.

MEETING THE SCIENCE STANDARDS

- Characteristics of Organisms
- Personal Health

MATERIALS

- reproducible page 44
- scissors
- tape
- colored pencils or crayons (optional)

Making the Book

1 Photocopy page 44. Cut out the two patterns along the outer solid black lines.

2 Turn the large piece over and fold down the two top flaps as shown. Next, fold in page 2. Then fold the title page over page 2.

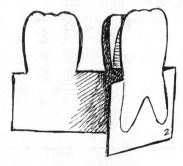

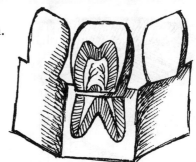

3 Open the book and tape the INSIDE ROOT pattern under the dentin.

Teaching With the Book

1 Ask students: "Why do you think your teeth are important?" (*Teeth chew and break down food into small pieces that can be swallowed and digested easily.*)

2 Have students describe their teeth. Ask: "Are all of your teeth the same?" (*no*) "How are they different?" (*Some teeth are sharp, while others have a flat, broad surface.*) Encourage students to draw pictures of the different shapes of teeth.

3 Invite students to color, assemble, and read their tooth books.

4 Turn students' attention to the back of the book. Explain that the picture shows 32 adult teeth. Young children start out with 20 temporary, or baby, teeth. At about age six or seven, baby teeth start to fall out and permanent teeth emerge. Permanent teeth include eight incisors—four upper and four lower front teeth—for biting, slicing, and cutting food. Four pointed canines or cuspids next to the incisors tear food. Eight premolars and eight molars at the back grind, crush, and chew food.

5 Ask students: "Why is it so important to brush your teeth?" (*Brushing helps prevent cavities and keeps teeth healthy.*) The extension activity below shows you how to use the book to explain to students what a cavity is and how it develops.

More to Do

Save Those Teeth

Make your own tooth book and hold it up in front of the class. Inform students that everyone has bacteria—tiny living things made up of one cell—in his or her mouth. Some bacteria stick to teeth and form a film, called plaque, near the gum and between teeth. Bacteria need sugar to grow and multiply. As bacteria multiply, they produce acids that eat away at tooth enamel. Take a pair of scissors and cut a little hole in the crown of the tooth in your book. Explain that the hole is a cavity, formed when acid wears down enamel. Cut the hole a little bigger, then a little bigger, to show that bacteria are multiplying. Open your book and show how the cavity is making its way toward the dentin. If the cavity reaches the nerves, the tooth will ache. If bacteria get into the blood vessels, they may cause an infection. Inform students that regular brushing and flossing help keep cavity-forming bacteria away.

Resources

❀ **Arthur's Tooth** by Marc Brown (Little, Brown, 1987). All of Arthur's classmates have lost at least one of their baby teeth. So when is Arthur's coming out?

❀ **How Many Teeth?** by Paul Showers (HarperCollins, 1991). Find out how many teeth babies, toddlers, kids, and adults have, then see how permanent teeth replace baby teeth.

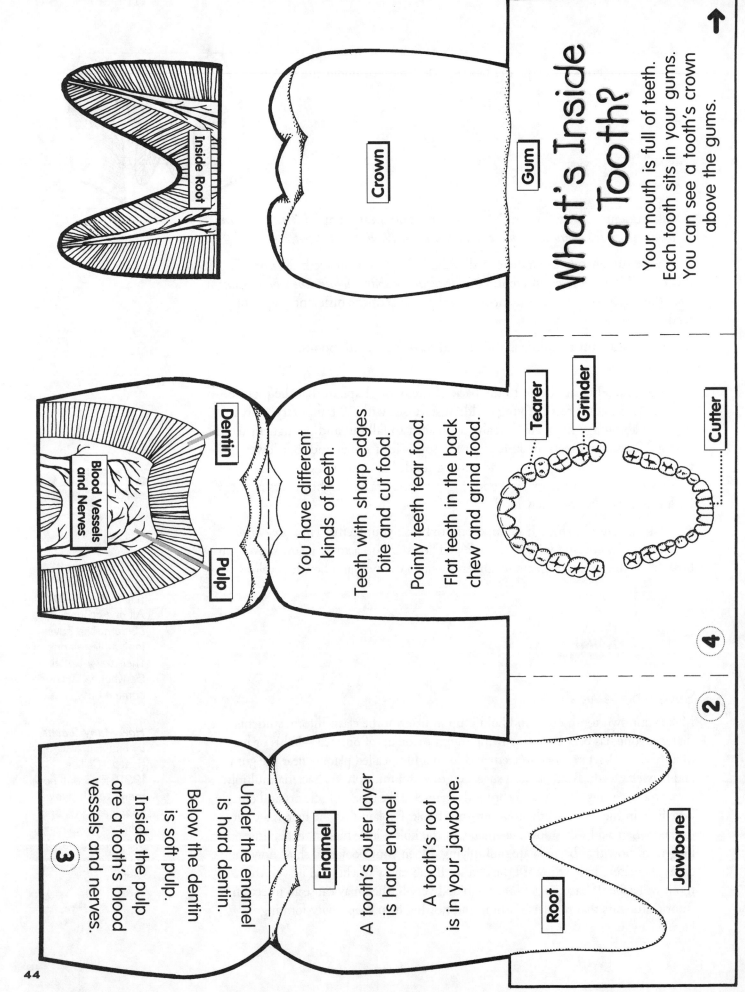

What's Inside a Tooth?

Your mouth is full of teeth. Each tooth sits in your gums. You can see a tooth's crown above the gums.

Gum

Crown

Inside Root

②

④

Tearer

Grinder

Cutter

You have different kinds of teeth.

Teeth with sharp edges bite and cut food.

Pointy teeth tear food.

Flat teeth in the back chew and grind food.

Dentin

Pulp

Blood Vessels and Nerves

③

Under the enamel is hard dentin.

Below the dentin is soft pulp.

Inside the pulp are a tooth's blood vessels and nerves.

Enamel

A tooth's outer layer is hard enamel.

A tooth's root is in your jawbone.

Root

Jawbone

The Body Book

Students learn how the different systems of the human body function.

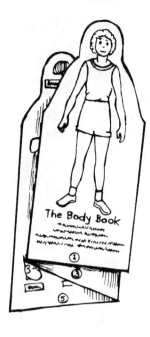

Science Corner

The human body consists of several systems that work together to perform specific functions. The skeletal system consists of bones that support the body and protect various organs. The muscular system allows the body to move. The brain, spinal cord, and nerves make up the nervous system—the body's control and communications center—which coordinates the different systems.

MEETING THE SCIENCE STANDARDS

- Characteristics of Organisms
- Personal Health

Making the Book

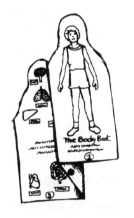

1 Make a double-sided photocopy of pages 47 and 48, or glue single pages back to back. The heads of the figure on both sides should be at the top of the page.

2 Cut along the solid black line at the top of the page.

3 Fold back and forth along the dotted lines so that page 1 is on top and page 5 is underneath.

Teaching With the Book

1 Have students lift their arms out to their sides. Ask students: "What helped you raise your arms?" (*muscles and bones*) Have students flex their arms to feel their muscles. Ask: "Can you feel your bones?"

MATERIALS

- reproducible pages 47 and 48
- gluestick (optional)
- crayons, colored pencils, or markers (optional)

2 Now have students feel their ribs and watch their ribs as they breathe in and out. Ask: "What do you think is under your ribs?" (*heart and lungs*) Inform students that the ribs protect important organs.

3 Invite students to color, assemble, and read their lift-and-look book.

4 As they read their books, encourage students to feel their own muscles and bones. When they get to page 3, ask: "What bone is between your ribs and hipbone?" (*backbone*) Explain to students that while bones protect the brain, heart, and lungs, only layers of muscles protect the abdomen.

5 Have students draw a line from each body part on page 5 to its correct place in the body on page 4. Ask students: "What do you think each body part does?"

✿ BRAIN: thinks and remembers; controls the way the body works

✿ HEART: pumps blood to all parts of the body

✿ LUNGS: breathe air; take in fresh oxygen and get rid of carbon dioxide waste

✿ STOMACH: helps break down food

✿ LIVER: stores sugar; removes harmful materials from the blood

✿ INTESTINES: small intestine completes the breakdown of food and absorbs nutrients; large intestine absorbs water and gets rid of solid undigested food wastes

More to Do

Working Together

Divide the class into groups of three or four. Assign each group a different body system (muscular, skeletal, brain and nervous, respiratory, heart and circulatory, and digestive). Help each group research and find out what each system does and how it works. Ask: "Does the system work alone or does it need help from other systems to do its job?" Encourage students to create a book or chart to present their findings to the class. They may wish to draw or cut out pictures from newspapers and magazines. Invite each group to share their findings with the class.

Hard Head

The skull protects the most important organ in the body—the brain. Cut out enough cups from egg cartons so that each student gets one. This is their "skull." Give each student two small balls of clay. Tell them that the clay represents their brain. Have students put one ball in a plastic sandwich bag, the other in the egg cup. Use a small piece of cardboard and tape to seal the cup. Have students carry both their "brains" in their book bags for one day. The following day, have students take out their "brains." What happened to each one? (*Most likely, the clay in the plastic bag will be crushed, while the one in the egg cup will retain its original shape.*) Discuss with students the importance of wearing a helmet when biking or skating.

The Body Book

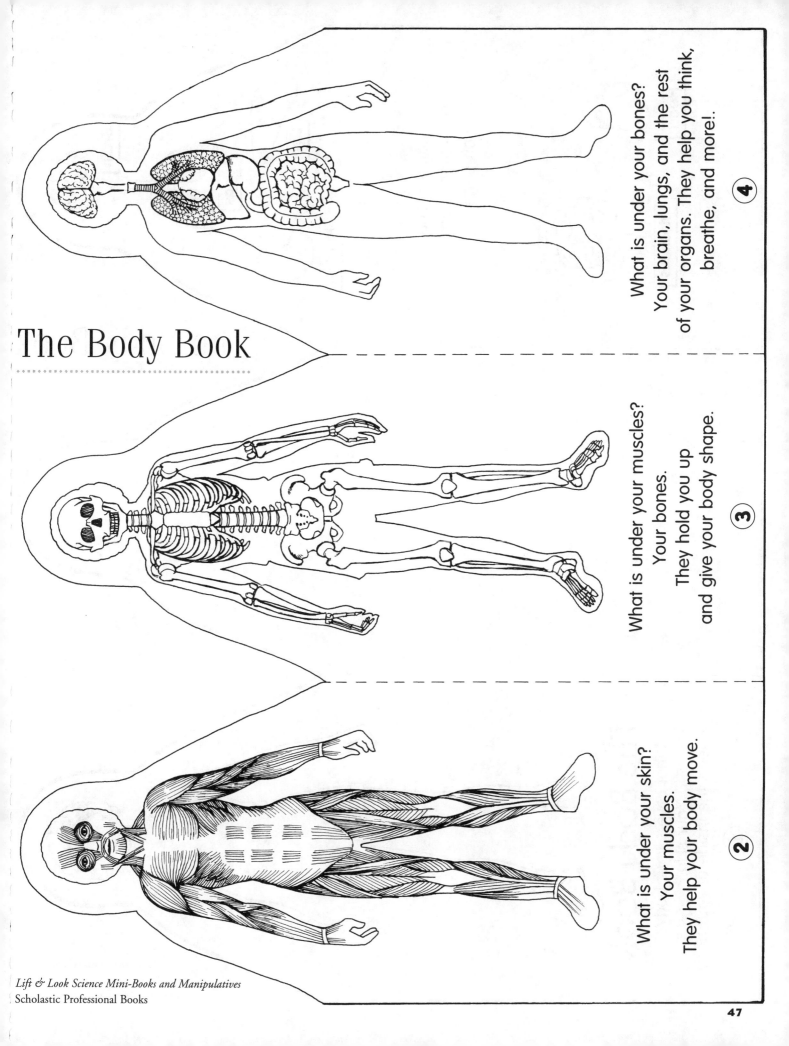

What is under your bones?
Your brain, lungs, and the rest
of your organs. They help you think,
breathe, and more!.

④

What is under your muscles?
Your bones.
They hold you up
and give your body shape.

③

What is under your skin?
Your muscles.
They help your body move.

②

Lift & Look Science Mini-Books and Manipulatives
Scholastic Professional Books

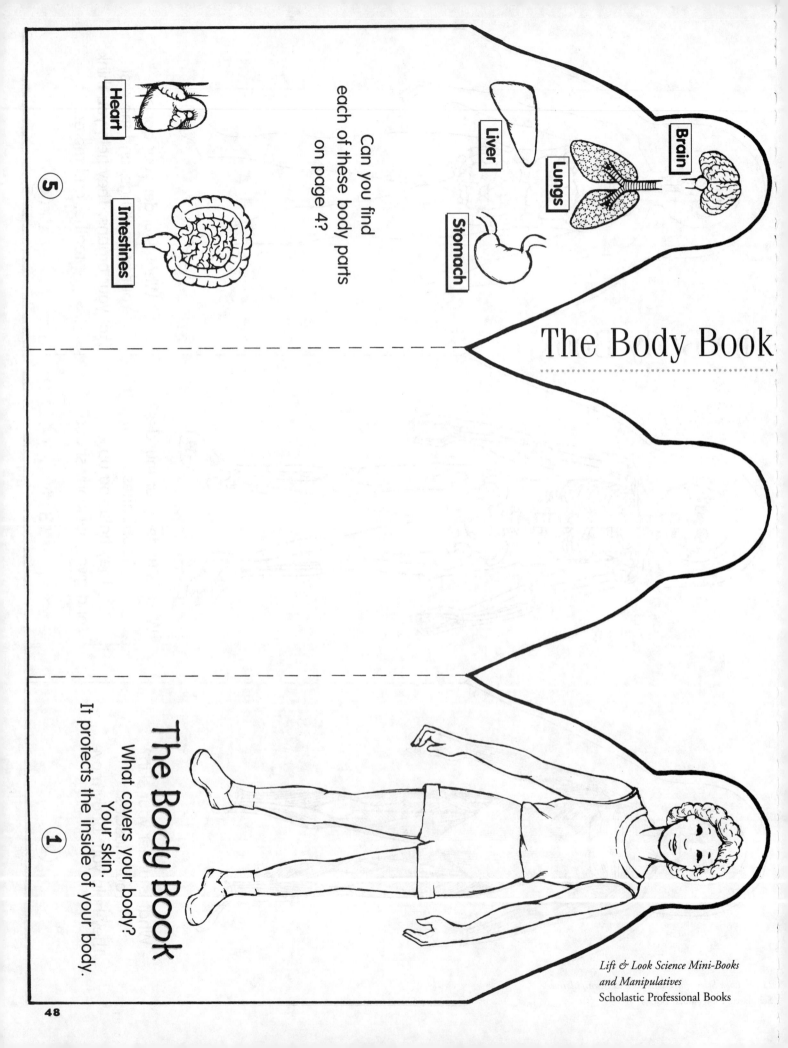

5

Can you find
each of these body parts
on page 4?

Liver

Lungs

Brain

Stomach

Heart

Intestines

The Body Book

1

The Body Book

What covers your body?
Your skin.
It protects the inside of your body.

*Lift & Look Science Mini-Books
and Manipulatives*
Scholastic Professional Books

What Will the Weather Be?

Students learn about clouds and the weather they bring.

Science Corner

Clouds form when water vapor (water in its gaseous state) condenses around specks of dust and forms tiny water droplets. When the droplets come together and grow large enough, they fall as rain or snow. Clouds are grouped according to their shape and altitude. Puffy, white, fair-weather clouds are called cumulus. Low, gray clouds are called stratus, or nimbostratus if they bring rain. (*Nimbus* means "rain" or "rain cloud.") Towering thunderclouds are called cumulonimbus. These clouds produce violent storms with lightning, thunder, strong winds, heavy rain, and sometimes hail. Different cloud types signal weather conditions fairly consistently. However, when making forecasts, meteorologists also consider wind direction, the presence of warm and cold fronts, temperature, barometric pressure, humidity, and how clouds change over time.

MEETING THE SCIENCE STANDARDS

◎ Changes in the Earth and Sky
◎ Objects in the Sky
◎ Properties of Earth Materials

Making the Book

1 Photocopy pages 51 and 52. Cut out the patterns along the outer solid black lines.

2 Cut along the solid black lines on the title page (page 51) to open the flaps.

3 Fold both patterns along the center dotted lines. Slide folded page 2 inside the folded title page.

MATERIALS

◎ reproducible pages 51 and 52
◎ scissors
◎ tape
◎ cotton puffs (optional)
◎ paints and brushes
◎ glue (optional)

4 Tape all the sheets together in the middle as shown. Be careful not to tape down a flap.

5 OPTIONAL: Glue cotton puffs over the clouds on the front side of the book. Paint the clouds on the other side of the book according to the description on the page.

Teaching With the Book

1 Challenge students to think about how the weather affects their everyday lives. (*The weather affects what they wear, what they do, and sometimes even where they can go.*) List students' responses on the chalkboard.

2 Ask students: "How do you think people find out what the weather will be?" (*They look outside, listen to weather reports, read about the weather in newspapers and on the Internet, and so on.*) Explain to students that in the past, sailors and farmers have relied on cloud shapes and movements to tell them what the weather will be.

3 Invite students to color, assemble, and read their books.

4 Ask students: "Which of the clouds in your books have you seen recently? What was the weather like after you saw those clouds?"

5 Inform students that observing clouds is just one way to predict the weather. Meteorologists (weather scientists) use a variety of instruments, such as barometers (which measure air pressure) and anemometers (which measure wind speed), to predict the weather. But even with recent technological advancements, including computers and high-tech radar, meteorologists still cannot accurately predict the weather all the time.

More to Do

Weather Report

Help students create a cloud poster. On a large sheet of posterboard, create a chart with five columns. Label the first column "DATE," the second, "CLOUDS WE SAW," the third, "THE WEATHER RIGHT NOW," the fourth, "OUR WEATHER PREDICTION," and the last column, "WHAT THE WEATHER WAS LIKE." For the next two weeks, take the class outdoors every morning to observe the sky. When they return to the classroom, invite students to fill in the first four columns of the class chart. The next morning, have students fill in the fifth column. How accurate were students' weather predictions, based on their cloud observations?

What Will the Weather Be?

Look for clouds.
They can help you
make a prediction.

No clouds

Prediction

Prediction

Patchy, fluffy
white clouds

Prediction

Giant, high, dark
clouds with thunder
and lightning

Prediction

Low, gray clouds
that cover the sky

Prediction

❸

Chance of a thunderstorm

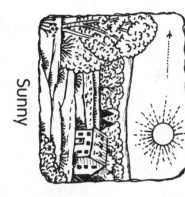

Sunny

Chance of rain or snow

Fair weather

Lift & Look Science Mini-Books and Manipulatives   Scholastic Professional Books

Exploding Volcano

Students make a flap book and observe
what happens when a volcano explodes.

Science Corner

Volcanoes erupt in different ways. The volcano in the lift-and-look book explodes violently and shoots a fountain of lava into the air. (Note: Inside a volcano, hot, melted rock and gases are called magma. When magma flows out of a volcano it is called lava.) As lava cools in the air, it can solidify into powdery ash, chunky stones, and bowling-ball-size rocks known as volcanic bombs. Lava flowing down the sides of the volcano also hardens into rock, adding a new layer that can make the volcano grow into a mountain over time. Some volcanoes erupt and then lie dormant for hundreds of years. Other volcanoes continuously erupt and spew lava but don't explode violently.

MEETING THE SCIENCE STANDARDS

- Changes in the Earth and Sky
- Properties of Earth Materials

Making the Book

1 Photocopy page 55. Cut out the three pieces along the solid black lines. Cut open the flap along the solid black lines on the title page, too.

2 Fold page 2 along the dotted line. Place the PULL HERE piece faceup behind page 2 as shown.

3 Fold the title page over page 2 and tape as shown.

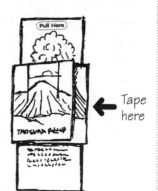

Tape here

MATERIALS

- reproducible page 55
- scissors
- tape
- colored pencils, crayons, or markers (optional)
- tiny pebbles (optional)
- glue (optional)

Resources

❋ *The Magic School Bus Blows Its Top* by Joanna Cole (Scholastic, 1996). Ms. Frizzle's students witness an erupting underwater volcano, which gives birth to a new island.

❋ *Volcanoes* by Seymour Simon (Mulberry Books, 1995). Not all volcanoes look like mountains—some are just plain holes in the ground. Includes pictures of volcanoes from around the world.

4 Open the flap on the title page and tape the remaining piece on the back of the flap so that you can read it.

5 **OPTIONAL:** Glue tiny pebbles on top of the small round circles under the ash cloud on the PULL HERE piece and on page 2 above the exploding volcano.

Teaching With the Book

1 Find out if students have ever seen an exploding volcano in a movie or on TV. Invite students to describe what they remember most about volcanoes.

2 Inform students that a volcano is an opening in the earth's rocky outer layer, or crust, where hot, melted rock can escape from inside the earth. Volcano is also the name given to mountains that build up around such openings.

3 Invite students to color and assemble their lift-and-look flap book. If students glued tiny pebbles to their book, point out that they represent the lava that cooled and hardened into rock.

4 Students should read their books as follows: first, the text at the bottom of the PULL HERE piece, then the text on the inside of the flap.

5 Have students compare the volcano before and after the explosion. Ask: "What do you notice about the volcano after the explosion?" (*The cone-shaped top of the mountain is gone.*) Explain to students that when a volcano "blows its top," the bowl-shaped pit that is left is called a crater.

6 On the back of their book, invite students to draw a picture or write a sentence that tells something they learned about volcanoes.

More to Do

Magma on the Move

Demonstrate for students how magma under pressure pushes out of the ground through a volcano. Place a half-full tube of toothpaste (with the cap on) on a desk. Ask students to imagine that the tube is the surface of the earth. The toothpaste inside is the hot, melted magma underground. Distribute the toothpaste evenly in the tube. Then use a pin to make a tiny hole near the bottom. Ask students what the hole might represent. (*a volcano's opening*) Press down on the tube near the cap. Ask students what this action might represent. (*magma under pressure*) What happens? (*The magma oozes out of the volcano.*)

Exploding Volcano

Pull Here

This mountain is a volcano.
Inside are hot, melted rock
and gases, called magma.
Magma can make a volcano explode.
Pull this piece up, then lower the flap.

Cut out

The volcano explodes.
Hot, melted rock shoots
up into the air.
It is now called lava.
When lava cools, it can
harden into chunks of rock
that fall to the ground.

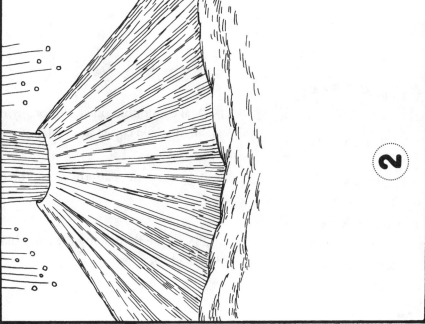

Exploding Volcano

2

How Are the Seasons Changing?

Students investigate what some animals do during each season.

Science Corner

Earth is tilted about 23.5 degrees on its axis. As Earth revolves around the sun, parts of the globe are tilted toward the sun, while others are tilted away. This is why we experience seasons. Places in Earth's mid to high latitudes experience four seasons because these are where the greatest changes in sunlight and temperature occur. To survive in these areas, animals need to be able to adapt to the changing seasons. For example, some animals migrate to warmer climates when winter comes, while others hibernate. In the spring migrating animals move back to their feeding grounds, where the food supply is plentiful during the warm season.

MEETING THE SCIENCE STANDARDS

◎ Changes in the Earth and Sky

◎ Objects in the Sky

MATERIALS

◎ reproducible pages 59 and 60

◎ scissors

◎ tape

◎ gluestick (optional)

◎ colored pencils, crayons, or markers (optional)

Making the Book

1 Make a double-sided photocopy of pages 59 and 60. Or use the arrows to align single copies as exactly as possible and glue them together back to back.

2 Cut out the patterns along the outer solid black lines.

3 Cut the flaps along the solid black lines, using the pinch method shown on page 5.

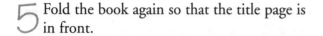

4 Fold the side panels along the dotted lines so that the title page and calendar months are on the outside of the book, as shown.

5 Fold the book again so that the title page is in front.

Teaching With the Book

1 Invite students to color, assemble, and read their lift-and-look flap books.

2 Have students look at the book's cover. Ask: "In which season are you most likely to see each of the things on the cover?" (*icicle and snow in winter; buds in spring; flowers in spring and summer; falling leaves and seeds in autumn*) Invite children to talk about their own experiences with the seasons. If you live in an area that doesn't experience the seasonal variations shown in the book, talk about the seasonal changes that occur where you live.

3 As students read, they will find four questions about what animals do in each season. Encourage them to use the pictures to come up with possible answers before lifting the flaps and reading the answers.

4 Have students look at the pictures. Ask: "Does the fall picture remind you of fall? What about the winter, spring, and summer pictures? How do they remind you of those seasons?"

5 Invite students to turn over their books and write a word in each calendar month that describes the weather or season for that month (for example, *cold, snowy, rainy, hot,* and so on).

6 Ask students: "What warms the earth?" (*the sun*) "Do you think we get more of the sun's rays in winter or in summer?" (*more rays in summer*) Try the extension activity on page 58 to help students understand how the earth's tilt on its axis affects the seasons.

More to Do

The Tilt That Counts

Push a pencil through the center of an orange. Place a lamp without a shade on your desk. Inform students that the orange represents the earth, and the lamp, the sun. Turn on the lamp and darken the classroom. Hold the orange at an angle and slowly walk around the lamp. Explain that the earth travels once around the sun every year. Have students focus on the lit part of the orange. Point out that sometimes the top half of the orange is tilted toward the lamp and sometimes it is tilted away. Then there are other times when the top half is tilted neither toward nor away from the lamp. When the top half (or northern hemisphere) of the earth is tilted toward the sun, it is summer there. At the bottom half (or southern hemisphere), which is tilted away from the sun, it is winter. When their positions are reversed, it is winter in the northern hemisphere and summer in the southern. When neither half is tilted toward or away from the sun, it is either spring or autumn. Ask: "What season is it when the northern hemisphere of the earth is tilted away from the sun?" (*winter*)

Temperature, Anyone?

Bring in a large outdoor thermometer to show your class. Inform students that a thermometer is a tool that measures temperature. Temperature tells how warm or cold the air is. Teach students how to read temperature on a thermometer using either the Fahrenheit or Celsius scale, or both. For a fun way to track temperature, use a zipper that is the same size as your thermometer. Glue the zipper onto a piece of oaktag, then write the degree numbers along the side. Invite children to zip or unzip the "thermometer" according to the temperature reading that day. Explain to students that as seasons change, so does the outdoor temperature. When days become consistently warmer or cooler, it is an indication that the seasons are changing.

JANUARY
FEBRUARY
MARCH
APRIL
MAY
JUNE
JULY
AUGUST
SEPTEMBER
OCTOBER
NOVEMBER
DECEMBER

How Are the Seasons Changing?

It's spring.
Days are getting warmer.
What does the robin do?

It's summer and it's hot.
Where is the turtle?

It's winter.
Brrr! It's cold.
Where is the chipmunk?

It's autumn.
The days are getting cooler.
What does the squirrel do?

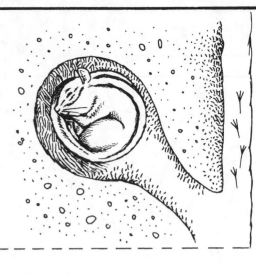

It hides nuts
for the winter.

It is asleep
in its
underground
home.

She builds a nest
and lays eggs.

It suns itself
on a rock
to warm up.

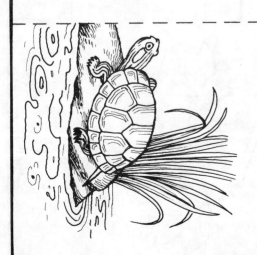

Lift & Look Science Mini-Books and Manipulatives — Scholastic Professional Books

The Changing Moon

Students make a moon wheel and observe how the moon seems to change shape each month.

The moon is Earth's closest neighbor in space. It circles our planet once about every 28 days. Unlike the sun, the moon cannot make its own light. The light we see from the moon is actually sunlight reflecting off the moon's surface and bouncing back to Earth. The sun lights only half the moon at a time. Depending on where the moon is in its orbit around Earth, different parts of it can be seen from Earth. From our viewpoint on Earth, the light reflecting off the moon gives the moon different shapes, or phases. When the moon is between the sun and Earth, its dark side faces Earth. During this phase, which we call new moon, no moon can be seen in the sky. As the moon continues to circle Earth, we begin to see more of the moon's sunlit side. First we see a sliver that eventually grows into a half-moon, then a full moon. After the full moon, we see progressively less of the moon as it is lit by less and less sunlight.

MEETING THE SCIENCE STANDARDS

◎ Changes in Earth and Sky
◎ Objects in the Sky

Making the Book

1 Photocopy pages 63 and 64.

2 Cut out the circles along the solid black outer lines on both pages.

3 Cut the flap along the solid black lines.

4 Place the circle with the flap on top of the other circle. Push a paper fastener through the centers of both circles to join them as shown.

MATERIALS

◎ reproducible pages 63 and 64
◎ scissors
◎ paper fastener
◎ colored pencils, crayons, or markers (optional)

Resources

✿ **The Moon** by Seymour Simon (Four Winds Press, 1984). Clear, concise text and dramatic photos give young readers a close-up look at the moon and its incredible features.

✿ **The Moon Seems to Change** by Franklyn M. Branley (HarperCollins, 1987). Easy-to-read text and simple illustrations help students explore the science behind the lunar cycle.

✿ **The Nine Planets** www.seds.org/nine planets/nineplanets/ nineplanets.html Invite children to get a close-up look at the moon, the sun, and the nine planets.

✿ **Papa, Please Get the Moon for Me** by Eric Carle (Simon & Schuster, 1991). A young girl who wants to play with the moon must wait for it to get smaller before her father can pluck it from the sky.

Teaching With the Book

1 Invite students to draw what the moon looked like the last time they saw it. Have students hold up their drawings and compare them. If all students drew only one phase of the moon (for example, full moon), draw other phases (crescent or quarter moon) on the chalkboard and ask if anyone has ever seen the moon look like those shapes. Ask students: "Why do you think the moon seems to change shape?" (*Answers will vary. Children may think that the moon actually grows and shrinks. The reason we see moon phases is a difficult concept for young children to grasp. The goal of this activity is simply to have children observe how the moon changes. This will lay the foundation for a more complete understanding of this concept in later grades.*)

2 Invite students to color and assemble their circle books.

3 The book shows the moon's phases over 28 days. Find out what phase the moon is in on the day your students make their books. (Check a calendar or daily newspaper.) Then have students match the big arrow on the flap to the moon's present phase. Invite students to lift the flap to see what the moon looks like.

4 Let students study a calendar or daily newspaper that shows the phases of the moon. Have students compare the information in these sources with that in their circle books. Challenge students to follow the moon cycle for the next 28 days using their circle books.

More to Do

Moon Match

Place a ball on a desk and tell students that the ball represents the moon. Pretend to be the sun by shining a flashlight on the ball. Darken the classroom. Invite students to stand behind you and look at the ball. They will see that half of it is lit. Have students slowly walk around the ball. The portion of the ball that is lit will change as they walk around it. Challenge them to match the lit shapes on the ball to the changing shapes of the moon in their circle books.

Sizing Up the Moon

When the full moon is low in the sky, it looks very big. Later, when it has moved higher, the moon looks smaller. Does the moon change its size? Students can find out. On the next full moon, give each student a large paper clip. Help them open the paper clip into a "V" shape. Tell students that soon after sunset, they should go outside with an adult and find the moon. It should be low on the horizon. Have them hold the V up to the sky at arm's length so that the moon is inside the V. Bend the sides of the V so the moon fits inside. About two hours later, when the moon is higher in the sky, have students look at it again. Use the V to measure the moon again. Does it still fit inside?

The Changing Moon

The Changing Moon

Have you seen the moon
in the night sky?
Does it always look the same?
Turn the circle and lift the flap.
The moon seems to change shape. It really doesn't.
You see only that part of the moon that is lit by the sun.

FLAP

The Changing Moon

Bottom Circle

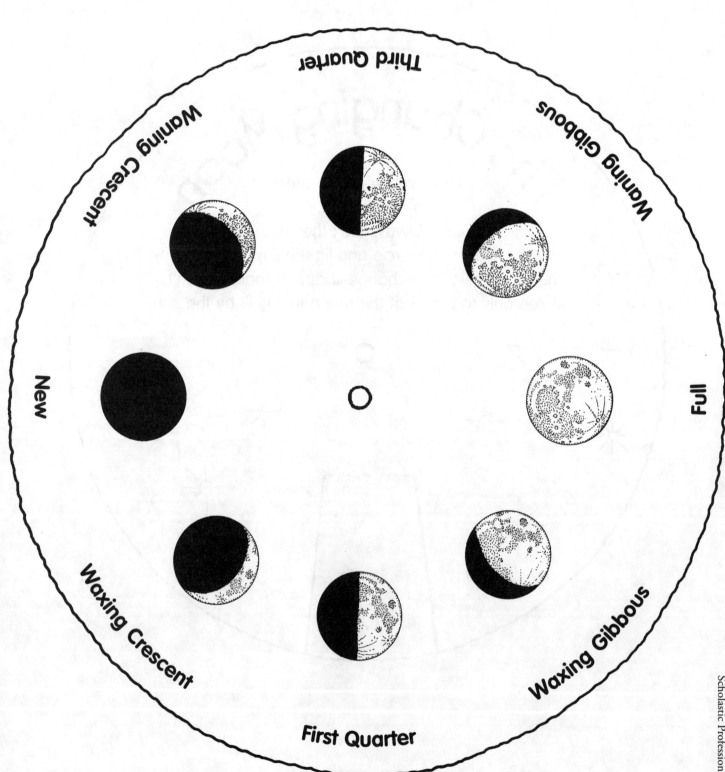

Lift & Look Science Mini-Books and Manipulatives
Scholastic Professional Books